READING CHAMPION

Cave Boy
and the Egg

by Damian Harvey and Bill Bolton

W
FRANKLIN WATTS
LONDON•SYDNEY

"I'm hungry," said Cave Boy.

"My tummy's rumbling."

"Yes, I can hear it," said Dad.

"I'm hungry, too," said Gran.

"What's for tea?"

"Fish," said Mum. "But it doesn't look very nice."

Everyone looked at the fish.

"Yuk!" they said.

"It's a bit smelly, too."

"Well this is all we have got," said Mum.
"If you want something else,
you will have to get it yourself.

Why not see if you can find some eggs,'
she said.

Dad got his spear.

"Come on," he said. "Let's go."

Cave Boy was happy.

He loved going hunting with Dad.

Not long after they left the cave,

Cave Boy saw a little bird

fly out of a bush.

"Look, I can see the nest,"

he said to Dad.

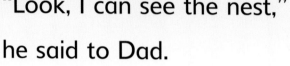

Dad looked into the bush
and saw three eggs in the nest.

"They are too small," said Cave Boy.

"Yes," said Dad.
"They are not big enough to feed us all."

Cave Boy and Dad walked on.

Soon they came to a forest.

They saw a big bird fly out of a tree.

"I can see the nest," said Cave Boy.

Dad climbed up into the tree.

"There are no eggs in this nest,"

he said.

Then Dad saw something
in a nest at the top of a hill.
"What's that?" he asked.

"It looks like an egg," said Cave Boy.
"A very big egg."

"That would be big enough
to feed us all," said Dad.
"Come on. Let's go and get it."

Cave Boy tried to pick it up.

Dad tried to pick it up.

But the egg was too heavy.

"We will just have to roll it home,"
said Dad.

"Good idea, Dad," said Cave Boy.
They pushed the egg
until it started to roll.

The egg started to roll faster.

"Slow down!" cried Dad.

But the egg did not slow down.

It went faster and faster.

"Come back!" yelled Cave Boy.

"We want you for our tea!"

But the egg didn't stop.

It went on rolling.

"Don't let it get away!" shouted Dad.

Cave Boy ran after the egg.

He ran as fast as he could.

"Stop!" he cried.

But the egg didn't stop.

It rolled down the hill, through the forest and all the way back to the cave.

When Dad and Cave Boy

got back to the cave,

Mum was trying to crack the egg.

"This is no good," she said.

"The shell is too hard.

We will have to have fish, after all."

Dad heard a noise.

"Is that your tummy rumbling again?"
he asked.

"No," said Cave Boy. "It was the egg."

The egg cracked open ...

and out popped a baby dinosaur!

The dinosaur grabbed the fish

and ran away.

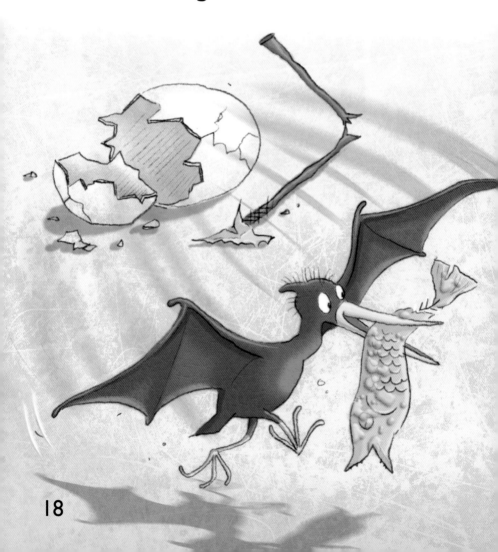

"So what's for tea now?" said Gran.

Story order

Look at these 5 pictures and captions.
Put the pictures in the right order
to retell the story.

1

The egg keeps on rolling away.

2

Dad can't find any eggs.

3

Cave Boy and Dad search for food.

4

A baby dinosaur grabs the fish.

5

Cave Boy and Dad discover an egg!

Independent Reading

This series is designed to provide an opportunity for your child to read on their own. These notes are written for you to help your child choose a book and to read it independently.

In school, your child's teacher will often be using reading books which have been banded to support the process of learning to read. Use the book band colour your child is reading in school to help you make a good choice. *Cave Boy and the Egg* is a good choice for children reading at Turquoise Band in their classroom to read independently. The aim of independent reading is to read this book with ease, so that your child enjoys the story and relates it to their own experiences.

About the book

Cave Boy and his Dad are hunting for food for the family dinner. When they discover a giant egg, they think they're in luck! How will they get the huge egg home, and what is really inside?

Before reading

Help your child to learn how to make good choices by asking: "Why did you choose this book? Why do you think you will enjoy it?" Look at the cover together and ask: "What do you think the story will be about?" Ask your child to think of what they already know about the story context. Then ask your child to read the title aloud. Ask: "What does the character name tell you about the story setting?"

Remind your child that they can sound out the letters to make a word if they get stuck.

Decide together whether your child will read the story independently or read it aloud to you.

During reading

Remind your child of what they know and what they can do independently. If reading aloud, support your child if they hesitate or ask for help by telling the word. If reading to themselves, remind your child that they can come and ask for your help if stuck.

After reading

Support comprehension by asking your child to tell you about the story. Use the story order puzzle to encourage your child to retell the story in the right sequence, in their own words. The correct sequence can be found on the next page.

Help your child think about the messages in the book that go beyond the story and ask: "Do you think Dad and Cave boy will go egg hunting again? Why/why not?"

Give your child a chance to respond to the story: "Did you have a favourite part? Did you guess what was inside the egg?"

Extending learning

Help your child understand the story structure by using the same sentence patterning and adding different elements. "Let's make up a new story about Cave Boy looking for food. Can you think of something else he and his dad might find for dinner?" What would they be able to find, in the woods or in a lake for example?

In the classroom, your child's teacher may be teaching pupils to read words with contractions [for example, I'm, I'll, we'll], and understand that the apostrophe represents an omitted letter(s). Find some examples in the story and ask your child to explain which words are represented.

Franklin Watts
First published in Great Britain in 2017
by The Watts Publishing Group

Copyright © The Watts Publishing Group 2017

Series Editors: Jackie Hamley and Melanie Palmer
Series Advisors: Dr Sue Bodman and Glen Franklin
Series Designer: Peter Scoulding

A CIP catalogue record for this book is
available from the British Library.

ISBN 978 1 4451 6182 2 (hbk)
ISBN 978 1 4451 6184 6 (pbk)
ISBN 978 1 4451 6183 9 (library ebook)

Printed in China

Franklin Watts
An imprint of
Hachette Children's Group
Part of The Watts Publishing Group
Carmelite House
50 Victoria Embankment
London EC4Y 0DZ

An Hachette UK Company
www.hachette.co.uk

www.franklinwatts.co.uk

Answer to Story order: 3, 2, 5, 1, 4